Patricia Kite   *Down in the Sea:*
THE CRAB

Telmessus cheiragonus (hairy horse crab) on sea lettuce (Washington).

ALBERT WHITMAN & COMPANY • Morton Grove, Illinois

To the Reverend Bruce and Lenore "Jerry" Button,
whose friendship has always meant so much to my family.

Text copyright © 1994 by L. Patricia Kite.
Published in 1994
by Albert Whitman & Company,
6340 Oakton, Morton Grove, IL 60053-2723.
Published simultaneously in Canada
by General Publishing, Limited, Toronto.

Library of Congress Cataloging-in-Publication Data
Kite, L. Patricia.
Down in the sea: The crab/Patricia Kite.
p. cm.
Summary: Presents the life cycle and habits of
the crab.
ISBN 0-8075-1709-7
1. Crabs-Juvenile literature
[1. Crabs.] I. Title.
QL444.M33K54 1994   93-21494
595.3'842—dc20   CIP   AC

Cover and interior design:
Karen A. Yops

The cover shows
Ovalipes ocellatus
(lady crab, Atlantic coast).

*T*hanks to Dustin Chivers, Senior Curatorial Assistant,
Department of Invertebrate Zoology and Geology,
California Academy of Sciences,
San Francisco, for his help.

Opposite: *Aratus pison* (mangrove tree crab) on mangrove leaf (Belize, Central America).
Above: *Cardisoma,* species unnamed (land crab, Thailand).

Look at this crab.
You can see two eyes on stems,
a hard body shell,
and ten jointed legs.
The two front legs have claws.
But not all crabs look exactly alike.

Platypodiella spectabilis (gaudy clown crab) on sea fan (Belize, Central America).
The second pair of walking legs is hidden from view.

Carpilius corallinus (coral crab, Bonaire, Netherlands Antilles).

Calico, coral, soldier, arrow,
ghost, swimming, toad, spider, sheep . . .
There are over five thousand types of true crabs
(crabs whose last two legs are easy to see).

Mictyris longicarpus (soldier crab, North Queensland, Australia).

Stenorhynchus seticornis (arrow crab) on sea whip (Caribbean).

Many crabs are green, blue, or gray,
but they can be purple, red, pink, white,
yellow, orange, gold, or spotted.

Opposite: *Dromidiopsis dormia* (sponge crab, Hawaii).
Above: *Macrocheira kaempferi* (imperial spider crab, California Academy of Sciences, Steinhart Aquarium, San Francisco).
Below: *Dissodactylus primitvus* (heart urchin pea crab). It lives in food grooves of the red heart sea urchin (Grand Cayman, British West Indies).

Some crabs are very large,
like this sponge crab and the spider crab.
A spider crab can reach twelve feet
from clawtip to clawtip.
That's the size of a small room!
Other crabs are very small, like pea crabs.
The biggest ones are only half an inch!
Some female pea crabs live in oysters.
They eat what the oyster brings in,
and they never come out.

Ovalipes ocellatus (lady crab) on seaweed (Atlantic coast).

Most crabs live in the water.
Some have back legs shaped like paddles
to help them swim.

Cardisoma, species unnamed (land crabs) looking for food at night in a jungle (Southeast Asia).

But not all crabs live in or near
oceans, lakes, or rivers.
Some live on land, even high hills
far from water.
A few climb trees!

Ocypode quadrata (ghost crabs) fighting (Cumberland Island, GA).

All crabs have claws on their two front legs.
Sometimes one claw is bigger than the other.
Claws are used to grab food, hold it,
tear it into small pieces,
and bring it to the mouth.
Claws may be used for protection
and fighting, too.

Uca pugilator (fiddler crab, male) using claw in courting (Cumberland Island, GA).

Fiddler crabs use their larger front claw
for sign language.
Each fiddler crab has its own "talk" pattern.
They wave their claws in circles,
up and down, or side to side.
Fiddlers from one beach may not understand
fiddlers from another.

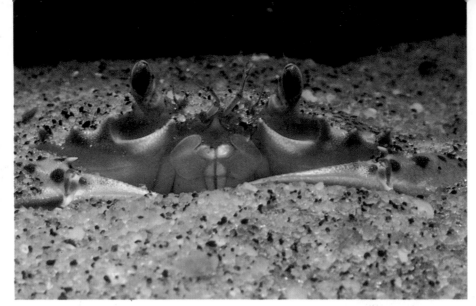

Callinectes, species unnamed, waiting in sand for prey to pass
(New Jersey coast).

Eyes

External
mouth
parts

Cardisoma, species unnamed (land crab).

Crabs have very good eyesight.
Their eyes are at the top of long stems.
Some crabs bury themselves deep in the sand
so only their eyes show.
Their claws grab food as it passes by.

Old hard shell

New soft shell

Callinectes sapidus (blue crab) molting, or shedding its old shell.
A crab can molt up to twenty times over its lifetime.

Crabs have a strong shell that protects them.
But over and over, as a crab grows,
the shell becomes too tight.
It splits, and the crab backs out
with a new shell that is very soft.
The crab hides until its new shell hardens.
Otherwise, enemies get an easy meal.

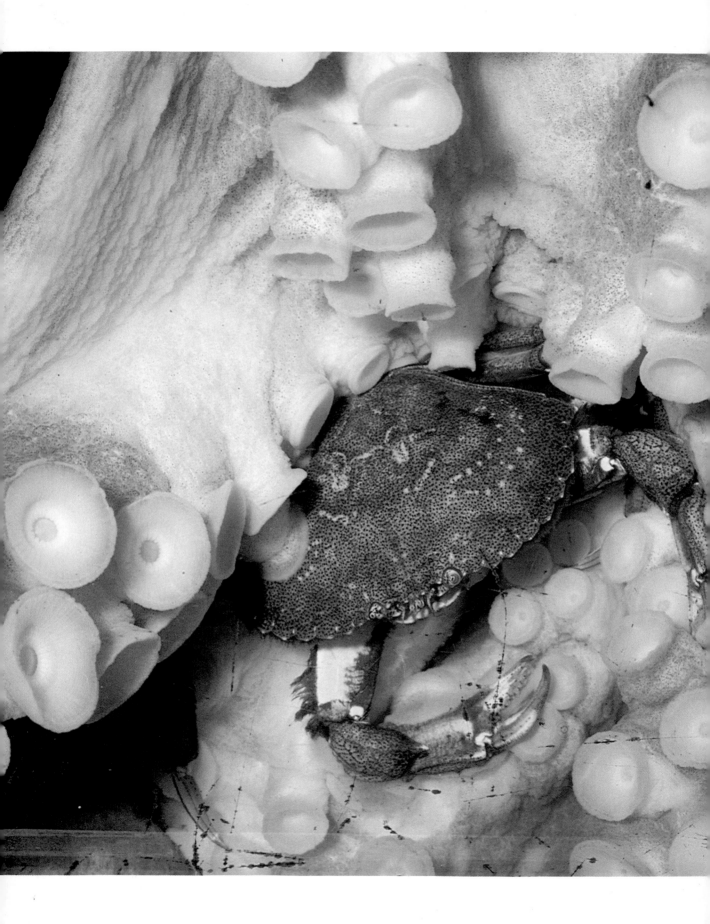

Octopus eating
Cancer, species unnamed
(New York Aquarium).

Crab enemies are octopi, fish,
sea otters, birds, dogs,
crocodiles, bears—and people.
Sometimes an enemy
catches a crab's leg.
It breaks off at a special place
while the crab keeps going.
(The leg starts to grow back
in the next shell change.)
Other times, the crab
does not escape.
If lucky, some kinds of crabs
can live three years.
Some live as long as ten.

Lybia tessellata (boxer crab) with sea anemones for defense (Bali, Indonesia).

Crabs protect themselves in many ways.
They hide in burrows or rock cracks.
One crab carries small stinging animals
called sea anemones in each front claw.

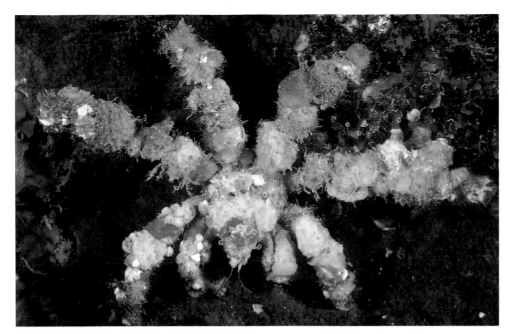

Crab of *Majidae* family (decorator crab) that has covered itself with pieces of sponge which it has clipped off with its claws (Micronesia).

Caphryra laevis camouflaged on soft coral (Australia).

Crabs may cover themselves
with algae or ocean sponges.
Other crabs look just like
the places they live.
Can you find the crab in coral?
Enemies would have trouble finding it, too.

External mouth parts

Abdomen

Paddl

Callinectes sapidus (blue crab, female).

If a crab is turned over,
this is what you see.

Grapsus grapsus (Sally Lightfoot) eating squid (Galapagos Islands).

Water crabs eat clams, seaweed, snails, and worms.
Land crabs may eat leaves and rotting or fresh fruit.
Both land and water crabs eat dead animals.
Many crabs are good scavengers.
This means they eat nature's garbage,
and keep land and water clean.

Liocarcinus puber (velvet swimming crab) with eggs
(Great Britain).

Cancer irroratus (Atlantic rock crab) releasing young into the water (Gulf of Maine).

After mating, a female crab will carry eggs,
from fifty to two million of them,
like bunches of very tiny grapes
under the front of her body.
Some kinds of crabs carry eggs for a week,
some for a month or more,
until the babies are ready to hatch.
Since all crab babies must hatch in water,
land crabs go to the sea each year
to hatch their eggs.
As female crabs enter the water,
the eggs break open,
releasing the young.
The crab babies swim away.

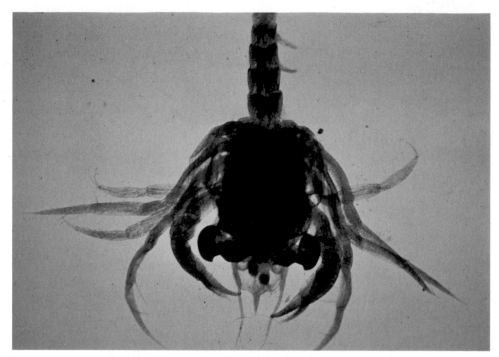

The early megalopa or larval stage shows true crabs evolved from a shrimplike or lobsterlike ancestor.

Late megalopa, the last larval stage before the young crab looks like its parents (Hawaii). The hairs cannot be seen in these pictures.

New babies are pinhead size, or smaller.
They swim using fine hairs like oars,
and eat sea animals tinier than themselves.
In about seven months,
the babies look like adult crabs.

Ocypode quadrata (ghost crab) in its burrow
(Horn Island, MS).

You may find crabs on a beach.
Often they sense you first.
Crabs can see you well,
and they can feel your footsteps.
So sometimes you only see this!

ABOUT CRABS

Crabs are part of a group of animals called *crustaceans* (kruhs TAY shuhns). They have jointed legs, four antennae, and a hard shell called an *exoskeleton*. Through fossils, their ancestors have been traced back nearly 200 million years. Lobsters and shrimp are also crustaceans.

All crabs have ten legs. This book talks only about true crabs. With true crabs, you can see all ten legs easily. Hermit, king, and robber crabs are not true crabs. They are *Anomuran* crabs. On them, the back pair of legs is very small and hard to find. It is often used for things besides walking. Hermit crabs, for example, use their back legs to hold the empty snail shell they live in.

Crabs sense food using antennae or feelers and also spot food easily because of their good eyesight. While some crabs bury themselves in sand or mud to wait for food to pass by, others go looking for food. The fiddler crab walks along scooping up muddy sand and swallowing it. The sand contains many small animals and plants. The fiddler eats these and spits out the sand. Sometimes you will see balls of leftover sand along a beach.

Scientists are very interested in fiddler crab language. Each type of fiddler crab has its own combination of claw signals, body movements, and noises made by rubbing legs together, striking a claw against the shell, or "drumming" the giant claw on the sand. Some also make noises that sound like growls, honks, and bird songs. Since different kinds of fiddler crabs—even on the same beach—cannot understand each other's languages, males can court only females of their own species. Scientists have found they can communicate with fiddler crabs by tapping on the sand in the same rhythm the particular crabs use!

Although some land crabs live very far from water, all must contact it regularly in order to breathe. Water crabs breathe through gills located within their hard shells. They take in water, which contains dissolved oxygen. Land crabs absorb water and its oxygen from damp sand or mud via strawlike underbody hairs. The gills of land crabs have evolved into a lunglike structure.

This book shows a scientist holding a crab. But it's best not to pick one up. Those pinchers can pinch!

PHOTO CREDITS: Cover: Animals, Animals/© 1994, E. R. Degginer; p. 1: Animals, Animals/© 1994, John Stern; p. 2: © Kevin Schafer/Tom Stack & Associates; pp. 3, 12 (top and bottom): Animals, Animals/© 1994, Zig Leszczynski; pp. 4 (top), 7 (bottom): Animals, Animals/© 1994, Capt. Clay H. Wiseman; p. 4 (bottom): © Fred Bavendam; p. 5 (top): Animals, Animals/© 1994, Mantis Wildlife Films, OSF; p. 5 (bottom): © Brian Parker/Tom Stack & Associates; pp. 6, 17 (top): © Dave B. Fleetham/Tom Stack & Associates; p. 7 (top): © Tom McHugh/Photo Researchers, Inc.; pp. 8, 9: © E. R. Degginer/Photo Researchers, Inc.; pp. 10, 11: Animals, Animals/© l994, Fred Whitehead; p. 13: © Tony Florio/Photo Researchers, Inc.; pp. 14-15: © Carleton Ray/Photo Researchers, Inc.; p. 16: Animals, Animals/ © 1994, Rudie H. Kuiter, OSF; p. 17 (bottom): Animals, Animals/© 1994, Kathie Atkinson, OSF; p. 18: © Noble Proctor/Photo Researchers, Inc.; p. 19: Animals, Animals/© 1994, Michael and Barbara Reed; pp. 20-21: Animals, Animals/© G. I. Bernard, OSF; p. 21: © Andrew J. Martinez/Photo Researchers, Inc.; p. 22 (top): © Biophoto Associates/ Photo Researchers, Inc.; p. 22 (bottom): © Mike Severns/Tom Stack & Associates; p. 23: Animals, Animals/© 1994, C. C. Lockwood.